TAKING THEM HARD

Steamy MMF Ménage

Michael Levi

ISBN: 9798814351975
Imprint: Independently published

1st edition

Cover design by: Michael Levi

CONTENTS

CHAPTER 1

I just finished landing at the airport. My next objective was to get to the gate where my plane would soon be at. I took my passport and ticket and checked them out, admiring them.

The destination was Raleigh, North Carolina. The airport I was getting out from was in Buenos Aires. I opened my bag and checked out other documents.

Some of them were from the college I studied in Argentina, and the rest were from North Carolina State University.

Thanks to a stroke of luck, I secured an internship to study there for one semester. A host there was also kind enough to let me live in his house. I'd never lived in another place before, let alone the house of a total stranger in a different country, so I was nervous.

I tucked all the papers alongside my passport and Visa back into the bag and headed out to explore the airport.

It was buzzing with passengers and planes coming and departing all the time. Chatter was as loud as the sound of the engines.

After some walking, I found myself a bit bored. I was sitting on a chair on the other side of the airport when I thought 'why not?' And grabbed my bag to head to the restrooms.

When I entered the restroom for men, I noticed the very clear and evident smell of piss and shit.

No matter, I still had enough time and was bored enough to ignore the unpleasant smell. I opened a stall and entered it without being noticed by the guys in there.

I opened my bag and grabbed my foot-long, realistic dildo. I'd bought it over the internet a couple of months ago and, ever since then, it'd become an important part of my life.

I couldn't have a boyfriend since I lived in a conservative family and neighborhood. The twelve inches in length monster was everything I had for the lonely nights.

It had all the bells and whistles someone like me could ask for. Playing with it long enough, it would blow a substance made of milk and honey that tasted and felt just like a man's cum. The dildo was expensive since it was state-of-the-art technology, but definitely worth the money I spent.

I put the dildo on the toilet lid and slowly took off my pants and underwear. Then, while supporting my weight against the walls of the stall, I guided my tight asshole into the fake cockhead.

I knew it wasn't going to be easy without some lube, but I didn't want to get myself all wet and oily before my flight.

First, I felt the tip of the cockhead trying to get in. It was fake and felt like silicone and plastic, but it was still very much enjoyable. I had to refrain from moaning when the first inch slid inside. It was rough, but waves of pleasure still intoxicated every cell in my body.

I pushed down farther and felt another inch coming in. More and more jolts of pleasure invaded my immature body.

My hole was shut tight around the plastic member. Once I had about half of it inside me, I started to slide up and down along its length. Powerful. Poised. Thick. That dildo was like magic.

I took more precautions when I started to slide more of the dildo inside of me. I felt it trembling and getting agitated when I had more than half of it inside of me.

Eight bloody inches were already occupying my rectum. Some people would think that it wasn't much, but for me, it was a monstrous length

I kept on pushing more of it inside until I felt it hitting my prostate. My body was trembling and shaking in pleasure. My cockette, much smaller when compared to the monster dildo, was hard and leaking pre-cum like a waterfall. *Shit, I'm gonna have to clean up the puddle on the floor later.*

My nipples, which were small and added to my overall skinny figure, were rock-hard. My body hair was erect when shivers ran down my spine.

My ass continued moving up and down, and I now felt little resistance.

My cockette blew a rope of jism to the floor. It was wet and sticky, and because of that, I knew I had to stop my fantasy right then and there. I didn't want to make a mess I wouldn't be able to clean later. I slowly and carefully got up on my two feet while keeping my hands against the walls. Then, I grabbed a piece of toilet paper and cleaned the mess that was on the floor.

I stowed the dildo in my bag again, put my pants and briefs back on, and then headed out of the stall. I looked around to see if I could catch any suspicious looks at me, but gladly, I didn't find any.

I hurried out of the restroom and then to the gate where the plane would be. I looked down at my watch and discovered that it was just about time for it to be there.

As I got there, I found a line being formed and got behind the last person. The plane was about to depart.

I slid inside it while fighting my way to secure the seat I had chosen for the flight. The plane was going to be packed. As I got to my seat and rested my head on the back support, I remembered that I still didn't know my host well.

So, I grabbed my phone and opened the browser app to access his profile that I had in Charbook. There wasn't much info on his profile, but from what I could gather, he was a man in his thirties who had a woman in her fifties for a girlfriend.

He also worked at a drugstore on the college's campus and had once been in the military.

As for his girlfriend, I found out that she came from a small country in the Middle East. She'd been living in the USA for quite some time already and was a professor at North Carolina State University.

I didn't find her attractive, but my best friend, who happened to be straight, said she was the very definition of a MILF. As I scrolled down her photos, I noticed that, indeed, he was right about that.

CHAPTER 2

After a long flight on the plane, I finally reached the city of Raleigh. It had a couple of high rises here and there, but it didn't impress me. I lived my whole life in Buenos Aires, so I was used to bigger cities with more people walking in the streets. The thing that most caught my attention was its cleanliness for a place that was a house for about five hundred thousand people.

Finding myself on his porch, I took a deep breath before bringing my hand up to knock on the door. I sent a message detailing my arrival, but it didn't seem that he read it yet. I just hoped he would recognize me from the photos.

His name was Lucas and, ever since the first time I saw his photos, I found out I had a soft spot for him.

I built enough courage to knock on the door and patiently waited for him to welcome me in. The door eventually opened and Lucas was finally in front of me in person.

He was a tall man – at least a head taller than I was, and well-built. I mentally salivated that handsome body of his as I checked him out from bottom to top.

"It's Mateo, right? Welcome! Come on in, please."

I slowly walked inside while checking out the interior of his house. From the outside, it was a two-story house that looked just like the others in the neighborhood.

"You can't even imagine how long the flight was. Still, being here's been enjoyable so far."

"Really? What do you think of the country and Raleigh so far?

Is everything according to your expectations?"

"Yeah, I like everything I've seen so far. The food isn't good though."

"Tell me about it. I've been living in this country my whole life and still am not used to the crap I have to eat every day."

I dropped my bag on the floor and sat on the couch. Lucas sat on the other couch and looked intently at me before asking, "So, wanna check out your room?"

"Sure, I'd like that. I want to change my clothes and put my stuff out."

Lucas guided me upstairs to my room. When he opened the door, I stepped into the best-looking room I'd seen in my life. It looked a lot better than the one I had back in my place in Buenos Aires.

"Hope you like it. I prepared everything for you. I didn't know what you liked and didn't like, so hopefully, everything is as according to your tastes."

"Yeah, it is. Thanks for prepping it."

"Alright, I'll see you later. I'm gonna make dinner soon, so I'll call you once everything is ready. My girlfriend, Alissa, will come here too."

"That's great! Can't wait to meet her"

Lucas closed the door and I fell onto the bed. I was looking at the ceiling when I started to reflect on what had happened so far.

Lucas looked so hot, but he was straight. *All the good-looking men are straight*, I thought. I just wished that my feelings for him weren't going to get in the way of our friendship.

When dinner was ready, he did indeed call me to go down. His girlfriend was in the kitchen waiting for me before we could eat. I kissed her on the cheek and started a long conversation about my arrival.

A favorite topic was my life in Argentina, which I was glad to talk about. I'd never seen someone so interested in my past life like that before.

Lucas cooked a couple of burgers for us to eat. We laughed off at the fact that my first meal in his house was a burger. Alissa didn't mind the fat food and ate it all while barely even stopping to talk to us.

She was sitting beside her boyfriend and was playing with him quite a lot. I noticed he had his hand on her leg and kept on teasing her. Meanwhile, my own cockette was hard because seeing what they were doing was hot.

He was much older than I was. I was just nineteen, and I did like older guys which made it all the better for me. Still, he was probably as straight as they came, so I knew I had no chance with him. Either way, a man could dream, which was exactly what I did as I contemplated him. Those long and big hands were of special delight to my eyes.

After we had dinner, I bid Alissa farewell and watched her get inside her car before heading back home. Lucas was in front of the house and accompanied me to my bedroom. We chatted a bit about me and his life in Raleigh before he headed back to his bedroom.

I had a busy day and didn't sleep at all on the flight to Raleigh. I was pretty tired and wanted to sleep a bit sooner than usual. So, I grabbed my stuff and headed to the bathroom, which was only a couple of rooms away.

When I got inside, I heard the sound of water coming out from a showerhead. Lucas was already in the bathroom and I started to step out to come back another time.

But then, he said, "There's another shower cubicle you can use here, Mateo. I had an extra one built just for you."

I went back inside while feeling a bit uncomfortable because he was naked. I fought against the urge to steal a glance at his naked body, even though I wanted to.

Then, I hurried into the shower booth and started to take off my clothes. I was feeling even more uncomfortable knowing that Lucas could see my naked body through the semi transparent glass.

I turned on the showerhead and the water started to come out a bit cold.

"There's cold and hot water here, Mateo. Mix them both until you find the right temperature for you," he shouted through the loud noise of the water.

I did as he suggested and found a nice temperature my body could get used to. As I soaked the bath sponge with foam and soap and started to massage my body with it, I heard Lucas singing from the other shower booth. The music and the way he was singing weren't even mediocre, but what piqued my interest was watching him naked when I knew he couldn't catch me doing so.

I was soaping my body slowly while I paid attention to the handsome figure that was hiding behind the glass of the shower booth. So tall… and elegant at the same time.

It was such a shame that he was straight and that I couldn't see every part of his body. My own cockette was hard and leaking pre-cum at that time. I wished so much I could suck his cock. *Sigh, these months here are gonna be so hard.*

Lucas finally came out of the shower booth and got dressed. I hurried to finish my shower so that I could go to bed early, too.

He got out of the bathroom and I left it a couple of minutes later. I totally hoped we were going to take many more showers together.

Lucas was just so dreamy! Even though I knew he was off-limits, I could still dream of having him just for me.

CHAPTER 3

I woke up and immediately opened the drawers to choose my clothes for the day. I chose a blue shirt and a white pair of shorts. Before I closed them, I realized that I hadn't brought enough clothes to live there. I needed to hit the nearest shopping mall as soon as possible, I thought.

I opened the door of my room and stepped outside. When I got to the living room, I found Lucas sitting on the couch and watching TV. He immediately turned it off and looked at me.

"So, wanna go downtown? Maybe even explore the mall a bit?'

"You just read my mind! That's exactly what I want to do."

"Great! Then, let's go," he said before we got into his pickup and he drove us to the shopping mall. It was my first time there, so I had a blast admiring the place and exploring all the stores it had. Lucas was happy to guide me and teach me some unwritten rules about being in an American city.

When we were driving back with all the clothes and shoes I'd bought, Lucas asked, "So, would you like to come to a party with me and Alissa? It's a frat party and probably very different from everything you know."

"Really? That would be so cool! I'd love to go there. I do need to make some friends here before classes start, so it's a good idea."

"Awesome. I'll call you over once it's time to go there. The party is supposed to start late at night when everyone is free."

"Great! I'll be in my room waiting for you to call me, then."

He took a deep breath, his expression changing. "Are you 21 already?"

"No, why?”

"Why? You really know next to nothing about the USA, eh? It's because the legal age for drinking here is 21.”

“Oh, sorry. I'm not. I'm only nineteen.”

"Not to worry. You can still have a lot of fun there.”

"I hope so!” I said enthusiastically.

Lucas drove me back home and I went to my bedroom to check out some stuff on the internet. My friends popped up on the screen and I was forced to talk to them. They all wanted to know what living in the USA was like.

At about 10 PM when I heard Lucas calling me from the living room. I was already ready for the party, and was wearing the clothes I'd bought at the mall. Lucas wore fancy clothes that were nothing like I'd seen in my life.

It served to accentuate his overall masculine figure. I was a girly man, so I stood a bit uncomfortable beside him. I didn't have much self-confidence, so that helped to make me feel out of place, too.

Alissa came as well. She wore a new and expensive pink dress. She said she'd chosen it because it had always brought good luck whenever she went to parties. I agreed that a dress like that one would probably catch the attention of a couple of other guys.

We both laughed it off. She said that nobody would ever dare to do that because they all knew what Lucas was capable of. When I asked her about it, she started talking about something else.

When I went inside, I was greeted by a bunch of burly men and a couple of girls about my age. The guys looked much older than they were and had thick beards that melted my heart. Lucas had one as good as theirs, but still, seeing those up close in full detail was something else.

The party was a blast. I had a lot of fun doing stuff that was forbidden back in Argentina. Everyone in the frat house was extremely interested to find out about me and what my life was like there. Again, I was glad to tell them pretty much the same I'd told Alissa.

Lucas, who wasn't his normal self anymore, came up to me

and asked, "Wanna come to the swimming pool with me? It's closed, but one of the guys here works there and has the keys, too. I figured you would want to be the first from your class to get to know more about the campus."

The idea was crazy, dangerous even, but even so, I still said, "Yeah, sure. I think that would be a good thing to do, don't you agree, Alissa?"

She was sitting beside us and taking a sip from her glass of wine when she heard my question. She was taken by surprise by it and looked at me with an inquisitive look on her face.

Then, she answered, "Sure, I'm coming with you as well. But wait - just the three of us?"

"Yeah, just the three of us, my love. It would be good to have some time away from them, just us, and without anyone else bothering us," Lucas explained.

I took one last sip from my shot glass and followed Alissa and Lucas out of the frat house. I could still hear the music and the chatter booming from there.

We walked across the campus until we reached the building that housed the swimming pool. Lucas picked up his keys and carefully opened the door for Alissa and me. He held it open for us gracefully like the kind knight he was.

We explored some of the rooms until we finally found the one which had the swimming pool. Lucas unlocked it and held it open for us like last time. I checked the corners of the room for any cameras, but gladly, there weren't any.

The pool was immense, but it had one downside: it was too deep for someone who couldn't swim, and that was the case for me. Lucas and Alissa jumped into the water and I stood behind them, watching.

They swam for a little while until they realized I didn't go in there with them. "Mateo, what are you doing? Come on, come here with us! The water isn't cold at all," Lucas said while swimming toward me.

The fright on my face must have shown him everything he needed to know. I felt useless being around two people who appeared to be proficient swimmers.

"I- I-" I started saying. Alissa, watching me mumbling, figured out what was going on and then said, "I don't think he knows how to swim, Lucas."

"What?! Why didn't he tell me anything about it? Come on, Mateo. I can teach you how to swim. It's not too hard and I'm a good teacher, too," Lucas said, opening his arms and coming to me.

I was still reluctant and uncomfortable about it, but I still decided to descend the ladder. Lucas was just behind me, waiting to envelop me in his strong and wide arms. Moments later, I felt his muscles crushing my delicate torso and making my heart melt again.

Lucas and Alissa helped me learn how to swim for the next thirty minutes or so. I learned a lot better with Alissa, thanks to the fact that I didn't find her hot. Lucas looked a little envious about it, and it wasn't surprising that he did.

Alissa was in front of me, holding me up by my armpits when she lost hold of me. I started to sink in, but then she grabbed me again.

Something must have happened that made her lose her balance as well, and then our lips connected all of a sudden.

I'd never kissed anyone before, much less a woman, but I didn't end it right away. Likewise, she didn't move away from me. Her lips were soft and melted my heart. We stayed like that for a couple of seconds until Lucas grabbed her by her shoulder and shoved her away from me.

"What the hell are you doing?!" He shouted at her face. I'd never seen him that angry before and was legitimately frightened. He grabbed me by the neck and shoved me away as well.

"Lucas, I'm sorry. I didn't mean to kiss her. She just fell on top of me and our lips touched, and that was all, really."

"It was way more than that!"

"No, dear," she tried to explain, "it was my fault."

"How was it your mistake to kiss him like that?!"

"It doesn't matter now anymore," she said while going to the ladder of the pool, "I just want to go home. This isn't fun anymore."

"Fine. I'll drive us back home, then," he said as he swam to the ladder.

He got out of the swimming pool and headed out of the room in a couple of seconds. Each step he took felt heavy on the floor. He didn't even wait for the two of us to leave the swimming pool, either.

"Do you think he'll be alright?" I asked Alissa before following her out of the room. She looked at me inquisitively and answered, "Yeah, he'll be. Just give him some time. He needs to cool off right now."

"I hope you're right," I said before opening the front door of the building which housed the swimming pool. Lucas was already far away from us and close to his pickup truck. We hurried to get to him, but when we did, he was already seated behind the steering wheel. The vehicle's engine was turned on.

He didn't say a single word when we entered his pickup. Alissa decided to sit beside him, and I sat in the back seat just like last time. None of us knew what to say, so the whole trip back home was awkward and tense.

When I got inside the house, I didn't say anything and just headed to my bedroom. I locked the door and plopped onto my bed. The last thing I wanted was to think about the implications of having already fucked everything on my second day in America.

However, my mind still couldn't help but think back to that horrible moment in the swimming pool. I'd kissed a woman that was a total MILF, and her kiss was a good one, but I had also just made a new enemy. That was, unless Lucas overlooked it, which I doubted he would.

The truth was that I had kissed his woman. She was old and definitely not my type, even though she was a total MILF, but Lucas would never understand I didn't feel anything for her.

What I wanted was him, but even if I externalized that to him, he would probably just get even angrier.

CHAPTER 4

I hadn't seen Lucas the whole day. I spent the whole time in my room looking outside and studying on my computer. Gladly, I got the password for the Wi-Fi the day before, because I wouldn't have the guts to talk to him after what happened last night. He obviously still remembered all the details, given that he didn't even try to talk to me.

At night, I went to the bathroom to take a shower. I half expected Lucas to be there, but was happily surprised when I found out that he wasn't. The place was clean and tidy. There were no signs of it having been used recently.

I thought I was in luck for not finding him there. I wondered what he was doing and if he was even in the house, but then my mind was soon more worried about other things, like what my first day of classes was going to be like.

I entered the shower booth and turned the water on. It wasn't hot or cold like the other times. It was nicely massaging the back of my neck while I thought about what my next day was going to be like. I hoped, more than anything, that Lucas wasn't going to kick me out of the house. I didn't have another place to stay, after all.

As I thought about those things, I heard the door to the bathroom being opened.

It was Lucas and he caught me when I was least expecting his presence! I was so startled that even the bath sponge slipped out of my hand and fell onto the floor. I reached out with my hand and picked it up before it was too late.

Lucas strode from the door toward the other shower booth without saying anything. *He doesn't like me anymore.* I felt awful as I realized I fucked up another friendship.

He turned on the showerhead and started taking his shower. I slowly took mine while I stole glances at him. I couldn't help but admire the strong and tall man that he was. *So out of my league, and yet, so close as well.*

While I was taking my shower and getting ready to be finished there, I heard the other shower booth door being opened. Lucas was stepping out and coming where I was. I was startled by that and let the bath sponge slip out of my hand again.

I was in complete shock when he opened the door to my shower booth and stepped in. He didn't say anything. He was just standing in front of me with a serious look on his face.

I couldn't help but look at it and also at his flaccid cock. It was huge and meaty. Even though it was soft, it was bigger than my dickie.

"Lucas, what's going on?" I asked while stepping back.

"This. This is what's going on, Mateo", he raised his voice while stepping toward me. He was now only an inch or two from me. I felt waves of warmth coming from his body and making my dickie get rock-hard. It was fully erect in an instant.

"This thing right here", he added while grabbing my cockette with two of his fingers before stroking it, "is nothing when compared to mine. You can't please Alissa more than I do. I'm much better than you will ever be, Mateo. You aren't a man at all."

I was confused as to where all of this was coming from. I'd never seen a man with such a determined look on his face. It scared me, and also, turned me on. My dickie was leaking pre-cum like never before.

"Lucas, I already said that it was just a mistake! Just a stupid mistake that I regret, okay? I didn't want to kiss your girlfriend, I swear!"

Lucas was having none of that. He grabbed my chin and lifted my head up. Then, he kissed me all of a sudden and I just let it happen. I didn't expect it. I struggled in the beginning, but then, I gave in.

His dominance and strength were overwhelming. I couldn't unlock my lips from his. His tongue was all over the inside of my mouth. I was finally kissing a man for the first time.

He kept on kissing me for what felt like forever. I'd never experienced something so good that everyone I knew frowned upon. All the fear and tension just faded away.

But then, his lips disconnected from mine. I felt lonely and frightened once again. When I opened my eyes, I found Lucas getting his towel to dry himself off. I watched in astonishment as he then put his clothes back on and left the bathroom. *What the hell just happened?*

CHAPTER 5

I was in my room checking the screen of my phone when Alissa stepped in. I hurriedly sat on the bed and asked, "Alissa? What are you doing here now?" She looked at me as if she'd seen a ghost. Then, out of nowhere, she hugged me and rested her head on my shoulder.

"It's Lucas, Mateo. I don't know what's going on with him. He came to my house and said that he wasn't my boyfriend anymore. But, I love him! I've never stopped loving him. What I did with you was a mistake, yes… but a calculated one as well."

"What do you mean?"

"Oh Mateo, you are so different and cute. The first time I saw you, I wanted to kiss your soft and big lips. Where I come from… having more than one boyfriend or husband is common, so I was thinking about having the two of you. Being only with Lucas has been so lonely!"

"But, you do realize that people here don't take well to that sort of thing, right?"

"Sure, but just because I'm living here doesn't mean that I have to do everything they do. I'm still a woman from Estony."

"So what are you going to do now without Lucas?"

"I don't know, but I was thinking of you a lot", she said before kissing me. Her lips were soft and warm like that time in the swimming pool. I couldn't disconnect them, much as I wanted not to cause more pain to my host.

Out of nowhere, though, the door to my room opened with

force and Lucas stepped in hurriedly. There was a loud noise when the door slammed against the wall.

Lucas had an angry look on his face. I refrained from making any comments as he looked at me, and then at Alissa.

She walked toward Lucas and tried to hug him. He didn't move a muscle as her arms enveloped his waist. She was gazing at him and Lucas didn't even tilt his head down to look at her. His eyes were locked with mine.

I wanted to say something so that things didn't get out of control, but then Alissa stepped on Lucas's foot and shouted, "Lucas, I still love you! You can't dump me like that! Do you want to find out the truth behind my kiss with Mateo?!"

"Yes, just fucking tell me what's going on already!"

"The truth is that I love you, but just being with you hasn't been enough for me. I need someone else to make me feel complete. It's always been like that in Estony. You can't stop me from being me. You either accept me for who I am, or we'll never talk again!"

"I don't-"

"Don't say anything else, Lucas! Just kiss me!"

She lifted herself up using the toes of her feet and the two young lovers kissed. I felt uncomfortable being all alone there, so I stepped toward them and grabbed Alissa's beautiful butt. She moaned the moment I pressed my fingers against it.

Lucas glanced at me and nodded in approval. I thought he was angry at me, but his current behavior showed the opposite. I felt encouraged to continue what I was doing, so I put my head slowly closer to her ear, and then I started to nibble on it. The woman moaned once again in pleasure.

Lucas put his hands under my shirt and slowly started to take it off me. I responded by taking off Alissa's blouse. She had her hands on the silhouette of Lucas's big and thick cock.

Seconds after, she was on her knees and taking off Lucas's jeans pants. Her hands were unzipping and slowly taking them off. Then, she proceeded to take off his white briefs as well.

I was behind her with my hands all over the soft buttcheeks

she had. She was wriggling her ass for me.

I took off her skirt and shirt, which made her completely naked in front of me. Even from behind her, I could see her boobs. They looked so plump and big!

Even though I was gay, I felt I needed to play with her as well. I wasn't turned on by her, but by the big guy who now had his manly cock out of his briefs.

It was leaking his pre-cum in front of Alissa. She moved in closer and opened her mouth to take it.

"Yeah, Alissa, swallow everything like you did so many other times for me. That's how I like it", Lucas groaned while putting his hand on her head as an act of approval. She used that as motivation to keep on going and didn't stop for a second until his cock was fully hard in her mouth. She was slurping and sucking on it with a lot of strength and grace. I could see her long hair bouncing from one side to the other while Lucas tilted his head back and started to moan.

I moved so that I was behind Lucas and started to play with his buttcheeks. They were soft and warm to the touch. I opened them up a bit to start rimming his tight asshole.

I just wanted to please him as much as I could, even though I knew he was the alpha male here and that he was going to be the one fucking Alissa and me.

Alissa forced her lover to sit on the couch. Then, she used her hand to make me come and sit beside her. Lucas was holding his cock in his hand and looking at the two of us with a funny look of lust on his face.

"We should share this", she proposed with a strong accent in her words. It was the first time her accent sounded so present. I never noticed it before, and maybe it was because she tried to hide it from us. Shame. It sounded so good.

She was the first one to go. Her body was bent to approach the big and wet man tool that belonged to Lucas. He was wriggling it and giving it long and slow strokes as if to tease us.

It was working because I was salivating more than ever before in my life. I was constantly licking my lips as I contemplated and waited for my chance to please my host.

Watching her lips going up and down along his man tool was making me breathe hard. I could even hear their own hard breaths as well at the same time. Her hands were gripping his dick, and she couldn't make her fingers touch her thumbs. I didn't think that his cock was that big but seeing it now, I realized that my initial assumptions were wrong.

Alissa wasn't all over his balls as well, so I moved in closer by putting my naked torso by the side of his hairy legs. He put his hand on my head and started to caress it. I looked up as if asking for his approval. He looked down at me before nodding. I was happy with the confirmation I just got and wrapped my fingers around his massive balls.

They hung so low and were heavy as fuck. They were so warm to the touch I couldn't keep my hands there much longer. It was my first time with everything that was going on here, so I hoped the two of them, who were much more experienced than I was, would understand my clumsiness and lack of proper decision-making.

I stared at his balls while my fingers fumbled with them. Lucas wasn't looking at me anymore. His eyes regarded Alissa with lust, and I didn't think he could look at anything or anyone else right now.

I noticed his prick growing even bigger, which I thought couldn't be true, but the more I looked at it, the more I realized that my host was just one of a kind.

He was the alpha male I had always wished for me in life. *When I get older, I want to be just like him!* I thought with some amusement.

"Wanna switch with me, Mateo?" Alissa asked after releasing her lips from Lucas' gland. He looked at her a bit furious but calmed down when he realized what was happening. I moved to where she was as she sat on the couch. They quickly started kissing again. Lucas' hands were all over her big and beautiful breasts. They looked plump and ready to squirt long lines of milk. If only she was lactating...

I stared at his cock. It looked big and frightening. I tried putting a hand closer to it, but then I retreated it right away. It just seemed so… long and thick. My own cockette, which was hard as a rock, was leaking my pre-cum.

My heart was telling me to suck him right away, but the rational part of my mind was keeping me away from doing that. Lucas ended his kiss with his lover, looked at me, and asked, "What's going on, Mateo? Isn't this what you've always wanted?"

"Yeah, it is. Just forget it. I should be brave. I can't let my own mind sabotage me!"

Lucas resumed his passionate kiss with Alissa. The sound of their lips and tongue rubbing each other was enticing me to do more. I felt as if I was receiving doses of dopamine as the seconds passed. My heart was beating faster and faster. My lips, which were so wet a moment ago, were now as dry as the Sahara desert.

I took a deep breath, closed my eyes, and moved my hand. I felt it crossing in the air before his rock-hard cock was finally within my reach. I slowly attempted to envelop it with my tiny fingers, only to have the same result as Alissa's. When I had it within my grasp, I feared I was gripping something else. I opened my eyes to check on that, because I was a paranoid idiot, only to find out that, indeed, I had his big member in my hand.

No more sounds were coming from their playful mouths. I looked up to find out what was going on and discovered Lucas and Alissa looking down at me. They had wide smiles across their faces. And then they both giggled before Alissa said, "Is this your first time, Mateo?"

I gulped in shame with my head tilted down. I felt some tears coming out of my eyes. I was feeling extremely uncomfortable, knowing that they were aware I didn't know anything about sex.

"Yes, I… am", I finally answered before releasing his cock from my hand. Lucas immediately grabbed it and put it back in it. I looked up in surprise, and he said, "Come on, Mateo. Stop being such an idiot with these things. We were all like you once, okay? Sure, you're a little late for this, but it's no biggie. This is your night, man. Make it count!"

I took another deep breath to prepare my mind again for the unique experience I was about to have. There I was, with the big cock of a man much older than I was in my hand. I could finally lose my virginity. My conservative friends were nowhere to stop me this time.

I slowly slid down the skin that covered his dick. It went down gracefully, with almost no effort needed from me. I put a bit more strength in my hand and the skin went down a bit more.

His protruding veins were pumping blood with increasing pressure as I tried to stroke him with greater intensity. Lucas repositioned himself on the couch again, but I didn't refrain from keeping his cock tightly grasped within my hand. I felt as if it was becoming mine. Lucas seemed willing to let me have my way with him.

I remembered I still had my pants and briefs on, so I took them off in an instant. Lucas and Alissa applauded enthusiastically. I looked down half happy with myself, half feeling uncomfortable with my cockette. Lucas looked down at it and reached over with his hand. He stroked it a couple of times, which made me pump out a rope of jism on his hairy leg.

He, then, used his hand to get some of the substance so that he could lick it. And then he moaned, showing me that he approved of the taste of my come, and I never thought that was something I would be witnessing one day.

I closed my eyes again, but not before noticing that Alissa's pussy was leaking her orgasm on the couch. There was an enormous puddle of wetness on the fabric of the couch, and I couldn't stop noticing it.

Then, I slowly wrapped my lips around the gland of his member. It was big, and oh so very soft as well. He was an uncircumcised man and much bigger than the average American as well. I never thought that someone could have a cock that was a foot long, but he was showing me otherwise. He was one inch bigger than the biggest dick I'd ever seen in my life. Not even men featured in porn movies held a candle to him.

Alissa emitted a long moan of approval before blowing out the hugest load of orgasm I had ever seen in my life.

I was bobbing up and down along the length of Lucas's shaft with all the care I could muster. I felt as if I was dealing with a precious and delicate thing, even though I knew that it was anything but.

After some minutes of doing that and Alissa kissing her boyfriend as much as she could, I felt his cock throbbing. The feeling was similar to when I had my own orgasms, only that it was another man having his. The feeling was a bit alien, and I was even startled by it a bit, but then I realized that I actually needed more of that.

His cock throbbed one last time before Lucas started to squirt the first ropes of jism all over the back of my mouth. I was startled when it began to happen, but then I got used to it.

More and more of his seeds filled my mouth. It was like it was never going to end. Lucas had so much power in his balls that it was unbelievable. I never realized, until now, that a man could have so much sperm in his balls. Even the most experienced women like Alissa would be surprised by him!

I swallowed everything I could while making loud noises with my mouth. Lucas looked happy with my willingness to please him. In return, I was happy with myself for doing everything according to his desires.

Alissa grabbed her boyfriend's head before kissing him. He was taken by surprise, but then they were kissing as if nothing had changed.

She hurried out of the couch and got on all fours in front of us. She was wriggling her butt while she invited Lucas to come over.

Her boyfriend didn't need another invitation as he got off the couch and headed toward her with his still rock-hard cock held firmly in his hand.

Alissa was leaking a lot of her orgasm, which caught the attention of my eyes. While Lucas got behind her and guided his cock in, I reached out with my tongue to lick up her puddle.

Alissa looked back and giggled when she noticed what I was doing. Meanwhile, Lucas slowly pounded her ass. It didn't look that her hole was tight, though I imagined that it felt homey. I wondered if Lucas would have more fun fucking a more inexperienced ass like mine.

In no time, he picked up his pace. His cock and balls were pounding the much older woman. I knew that she was in absolute delight while her eyes rolled back. Lucas grabbed a handful of her hair and was using it as support to pound her even harder.

Meanwhile, I finished licking the floor clean of her orgasm. I was caressing Lucas's big and plump buttcheeks while he rocked his girlfriend.

He didn't even notice what I was doing while he did her good. They were both moaning and breathing so heavy that my dickie, which had turned flaccid after blowing the jism over the floor, was now fully erect.

Minutes later, Lucas' body trembled in pleasure once again. I noticed his cock and ballsack stiffening moments before he started blowing all the rest of his load inside her pussy. I wondered if she would get pregnant from that, but then I remembered that she was probably not on her period.

She lied down on the floor and Lucas followed suit. They were hugging and cuddling. I was panting a lot as the action finally reached its end. I wanted to get up to eat something, but then my legs gave up on me.

Alissa took my hand and made me lie down between them. She then gave me a quick kiss before I fell asleep in Lucas's muscular arms.

It seemed that everything was alright between us after all…

The End

The next page has a steamy sneak peek for a similar story. Go check it out!

Lastly, leave a review if you liked the book. Your feedback helps me improve my stories!

TEASER: INDECENTLY THICK

Straight to Gay MM First Time
Cheating and Shameless - 3

As a married man who just had my second gay experience, I was longing for more. My first time was with Mike, a gay cop who kept his true sexual orientation hidden. My second time was with my Dutch friend, and the worst was that not everything happened according to my expectations.

Donny, in the end, decided to stay with his cheating girlfriend. I couldn't believe the words that came out of his mouth when he explained his decision to stay with Danica.

"Are you FUCKING serious?!" I asked crustily at him.

"Yeah... You know better than anyone how much I love her, Lucas. What we did that night... it was just an experience."

"But I just can't forget it!"

"Lucas... don't you have a wife to go back to?" He asked before closing the door in front of me and leaving me alone in the hallway.

Daisy? FUCK HER. She's probably humping several men in a gangbang. I want you, Donny. When will you finally understand that?

Not only was Donny a good-looking Dutchman, but he was also kind and shy. I had a soft spot for people with low self-esteem like him. Plus, that accent of his… OH MY GOD, I couldn't stop thinking about him!

I was going crazy, especially because Daisy had called saying she wanted me to come back. I said, "Honey, NO. I'm not going back. I know you have already betrayed me multiple times. Truth is, I already did that to you. So yeah, it's better to end this. We should prepare the paperwork and never see each other again."

She then hung up on me and the next time we were supposed to meet would be to make the divorce official. I was kind of content that she didn't say anything else, too. As far as I was concerned, Daisy wasn't my wife anymore.

Anyhow, my biggest concern was Donny. I was pretty sure his girlfriend was cheating on him. I just needed to find solid proof – more solid than her online messages – to make Donny finally break up with her.

I had a special power that allowed me to shrink my body to any size I wanted. I used that power to spy on Donny when he was taking a shower, sleeping, using his computer, playing games, fucking Danica, etc. In other words, I was a camera constantly aimed at him.

I could use that power to get the proof I wanted, but even with that in my favor, finding what I needed would be a challenge. I'd have to find where Danica lived and stalk her until she met up with her lover.

Then, with my phone in hand, I'd take pictures and record her cheating on Donny. That would be all the proof I needed. I was very excited to start my plan.

Meanwhile, I would have to content myself with spying on Donny. Of course, he didn't know about my superpower. Nobody could find that about me because I'd be all over in the news. It was a gift given to me that required responsibility.

OTHER BICURIOUS SERIES AND MORE

SERIES - BICURIOUS GUYS

Love in the dorm, professors crossing lines, jocks swinging the other way, and more. This series is all about college steam.

1. Caught Looking by the Quarterback
2. Caught Looking by the Basketeer
3. Caught Looking by the Dropout
4. Caught Looking by the Jock
5. Caught Looking by the Roommate

SERIES - GAY FOR BLUE COLLARS

They are massive, thick, and their hands are extra calloused. These blue collars know no boundaries.

1. Given to the Cop
2. Given to the Miner
3. Given to the Plumber
4. Given to the Firefighter
5. Given to the Mechanic

ABOUT THE AUTHOR

Steamy MM stories, baby! Michael Levi can't go a day without sitting down and putting into words all the dirty scenes that sprout in his mind. His collection is diverse, but it's gay love only. And if you are looking for something free, check his mailing list. Warning: it can be extra spicy.

When Michael Levi isn't writing, he's chilling out by the lake close to his house. Nothing better than kicking back with a martini in his hand as he daydreams his next explicit scenes.